THE GREEN MACHINES
FLAMEKRAKEN
and the FOREST FIRE

For Theo, our ancient forests, and every creature that calls them home—J.S.

To George and Edie—P.C.

Flamekraken and the Forest Fire
Text written by James Sellick © 2025. Illustrations © 2025 Patrick Corrigan

First published in 2025 by Ivy Kids, an imprint of The Quarto Group.
100 Cummings Center, Suite 265D, Beverly, MA 01915, USA.
T +1 978-282-9590 www.Quarto.com

The right of James Sellick to be identified as the author and Patrick Corrigan to be identified as the illustrator of this work has been asserted by them in accordance with the Copyright, Designs and Patents Act, 1988 (United Kingdom). All rights reserved.

No part of this publication may be reproduced, stored in a retrieval system, or transmitted, in any form, or by any means, electrical, mechanical, photocopying, recording, or otherwise without the prior written permission of the publisher or a license permitting restricted copying.

ISBN: 978-1-83600-397-7
eISBN: 978-1-83600-399-1

The illustrations were created digitally
Set in Adobe Garamond and Modern Love

Designer: Myrto Dimitrakoulia
Editor: Molly Mead
Production Controller: Dawn Cameron
Art Director: Karissa Santos
Publisher: Peter Marley

Manufactured in Villatuerta, Spain, on recycled FSC paper GC042025
1 3 5 7 9 8 6 4 2

FLAMEKRAKEN
and the FOREST FIRE

James Sellick & Patrick Corrigan

It was another sizzling day in Evergreen Forest.

Kevin was teaching Kia how to climb.

Suddenly, a strong gust of wind raced through the forest. It blew flames from an abandoned campfire into a pile of dried leaves.

The flames from the leaves spread to a bush.

The flames from the bush spread to a tree.

Before anyone knew what was happening,
a whole patch of forest was burning.

WILDFIRE!

Fortunately, Flamekraken was patrolling the edge of the forest. He spotted the cloud of black smoke billowing into the air.

WILDFIRE IN EVERGREEN FOREST! he reported over his radio.

Along forest tracks, Flamekraken bumped and bounced.

Flamekraken soon arrived at the wildfire.

He scanned for anyone in immediate danger.

UP HERE!

OVER HERE!

DOWN HERE!

Flamekraken BURST into action.

With all eight hoses, he BLASTED water at the fire.

The blaze retreated but didn't stop.

The flames flickered and sizzled and crackled and crept.
Flamekraken FIRED his water harder and harder and harder.

He eventually got the undergrowth under control.

To make things worse, Flamekraken's emergency light began to flash.
His water tank was running low. His hoses were losing power.

OH NO!

Flamekraken wasn't going to give up hope.
He battled the blaze until his last few drops.
But he couldn't quite reach the tops of the trees.

In an instant, the fire was EXTINGUISHED!

I can always count on you, Heletor!

But the battle to save the day wasn't over. The fire had stripped Kevin and Kia's tree of all its branches. There was no safe route down!

We're stuck!

Heletor lowered her rope, but the wind kept blowing it out of Kevin's reach . . .

Luckily, Flamekraken had another trick hidden up his motor.

Out of his roof, Flamekraken extended his electric ladder. It rose higher and higher and higher, until it reached Kevin and Kia. Together, they clambered onto the metal bars and were lowered to safety.

Thank you!

Kia, Dixie, Sid, and Kevin were relieved, but devastated that their home had turned to ash.

Zooming through the sky, the drones rained down thousands of seeds.

Over the next few weeks, the Green Machines and the humans of Hope Island worked together to help the burned patch of forest begin to recover.

Grow, forest! Grow!

WHAT'S THE REAL STORY?

Wildfires are unplanned fires that burn in grasslands and forests like Evergreen Forest. Wildfires do happen naturally and are actually very important in keeping some forest ecosystems healthy. The problem is that in recent years wildfires have become much bigger and more damaging, and they are often now harming instead of helping our forests.

This is because of climate change. Hotter, drier weather can cause trees, bushes, and leaves to dry out, making them the perfect fuel for a wildfire. On top of this, people have cut down big, fire-resistant trees for timber, which has prevented many small, natural fires from happening. So when fires do occur, there is more dry wood around and the fires are extra ferocious.

To help protect our grasslands and forests from dangerous wildfires, there are several things people can do. We can be careful not to start them accidentally, such as with careless campfires. We can manage forests to protect old trees, and allow some small, controlled fires to clear out the extra dry wood. We can replant fire-resistant trees and shrubs after big fires. Some people even think it might be possible to replant forests using drones, which inspired Electrostorm in the story, although this isn't proven yet. And the biggest thing we can do is work together to slow climate change.

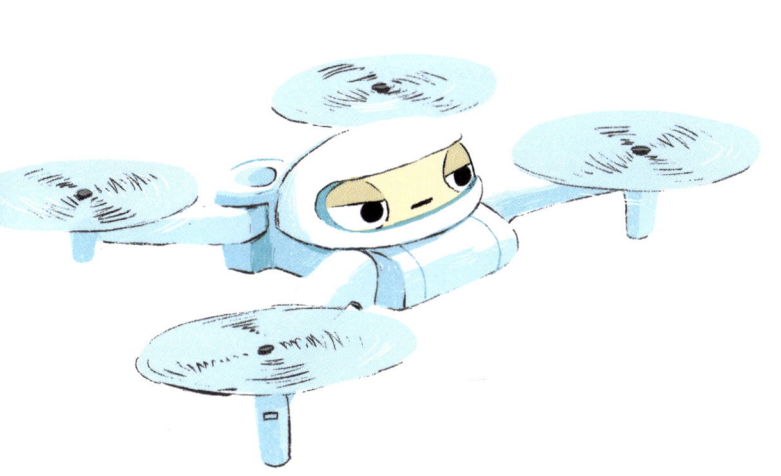

Millions of people are fighting to end the use of fossil fuels for electricity, heat, and transportation, which is the lead cause of climate change. Instead, they're demanding a greener future that is fueled by nothing but renewable energy. This means energy from sunshine, water, and wind. A healthier climate is what our ancient forests really need to survive for centuries to come.

Meet the Green Machines—the brave gang of vehicles working together to save Hope Island!

Also available:

Wave Warrior and the Reef Rescue

When Wave Warrior spots Codzilla dragging his net along the seabed, she is quick to confront him. After all, these are protected waters! But Codzilla makes it very clear he has no intention of fishing elsewhere. Will Wave Warrior have what it takes to stop Codzilla and save Hope Reef?

A final note to grownups:

In these stories, machines are the heroes—but in real life, technology is only a small part of the solution. More than anything, we need to demand that governments and big businesses take action to protect our precious planet.